Bad, Bad
BUNNY TROUBLE

Bad, Bad
BUNNY TROUBLE

by Hans Wilhelm

Scholastic Inc.

New York Toronto London Auckland Sydney

ISBN 0-590-47916-4

12 11 10 9 8 7 6 5 4 3 2 1   4 5 6 7 8 9/9

Printed in the U.S.A.   09

First Scholastic printing, February 1994

R̶alph was a bunny who loved soccer more than
anything else in the whole wide world. He could play
all day long, and he never wanted to stop.

"Ralph, come inside now," his mother called.
"You have to get dressed for your sister's
birthday party."

"Rats!" said Ralph.

It was the last thing he wanted to do.

"Look how dirty you are!" scolded his mother. "Quick, go upstairs and change. The guests will be here any minute."

Ralph saw that his mother was putting the candles on the birthday cake for Liza. She had also bought a coffee cake. Ralph wondered how it tasted.

Ralph was still angry at having to leave his soccer game.

"This party would be more fun if we could just play soccer instead of sing stupid songs," he grumbled. "We'll probably play stupid musical chairs or pin the stupid tail on the stupid donkey."

Ralph took his time getting ready. He was the last one to join the party.

After everyone sang "Happy Birthday,"
Ralph's mother was ready to cut the cakes.
Ralph said, "I want a piece of coffee cake."

"No, you can't have coffee cake," said his mother.
"It's for the grown-ups. The birthday cake is
for the children."

"But I don't want birthday cake! I want coffee cake!"
Ralph cried and stomped his feet.

"No!" his mother said again.

Ralph was so angry, he could not control himself.
He did something awfully horrible.

"If I can't have it, then nobody can," he said
—and he spat on the cake!

That did it! Now Ralph was in
bad, bad trouble.

"Ralph, how could you!" his mother gasped.
"Up to the attic, this instant! I'll deal with you later!"

Ralph's cheeks were burning as he stomped up to
the attic. But he really didn't mind. The attic was
the workshop where the rabbits decorated Easter eggs.
It was a nice big room, just perfect for working on
his fancy footwork.

Suddenly Ralph heard
horrifying screams outside,
and from the distance
came a terrifying chant:

"Tasty bunnies, hop, hop, hop,
Are delicious in the pot.
Simmered, boiled, or as a stew!
Watch out! Here we come for you!"

Looking out the window, Ralph saw
three large, savage foxes.

Now everyone was in bad, bad trouble!

Downstairs there was great trembling
and crying. The rabbits locked the windows
and bolted the doors.

Then they all went down into the cellar,
which was the safest place.

In all the commotion,
everyone forgot about Ralph.

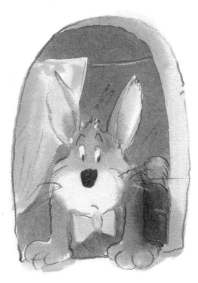

Ralph had to think fast.
He picked up a big basket of eggs
— and threw them out the window.

When the attacking foxes came running, they slipped and slid and skidded and toppled and crashed into each other in the gooey mess of broken eggs.

The foxes were not ready for this. Badly bruised and covered with slimy egg whites, they looked up and saw Ralph laughing in the attic window. They whispered among themselves and then disappeared into the bushes.

Soon the three foxes returned with a long, long ladder.
They started to climb up to the attic window.

But Ralph was prepared. He had lined up all the pails
of Easter egg dye, and one by one he dumped
them all over the foxes — first yellow,
then blue, then violet, and finally a big pail
of bright red dye.

This was too much for the foxes.
Grumbling, they slunk back
into the bushes.

"Victory!" cried Ralph,
and he kicked his soccer ball
across the room.

But in the next moment,
Ralph heard and felt heavy thumps.
Everything in the room started shaking.
Now what was happening?

The foxes were back! And they were still trying to get in.

"Thump! Thump! Thump!
We're coming through
To have a bunny barbecue."

Ralph knew that now he needed some help. He thought of Brutus, the bull, inside the barn. But the barn was so far away.

There's just one chance, he thought.

Ralph placed his soccer ball
on the windowsill. This would be
the most important kick he had
ever made.

Ralph gave it all he had.

The ball arced and soared
and disappeared into the
open window of the barn.

"Ha, ha, ha! You missed us!"
laughed the foxes and they gave
the door another big thump.

Inside the barn, the animals were enjoying
their afternoon snooze when the ball sailed through
the window.

It bounced off the rooster's tail.

"Yike-a-doodle-doo!" he cried as the ball
headed for the hen.

"Squawk!" cried the startled hen,
who accidentally laid an egg...

...which dropped on the pig and made
her little piglets squeal with laughter.
They giggled so hard that they
knocked over the milk can.
Milk splashed all over
the billy goat.

Shaking and trying to kick himself dry,
the goat woke up the sheep and scared them so much...

...they fell against the ladder, which toppled over
and knocked down the bales of hay...

...which fell on...

. . . Brutus the bull!

Brutus had a terrible temper
and he didn't like to have
his nap interrupted.
He broke through the pen
and crashed out the barn door.
He was so mad that nothing
could have stopped him.

There was only one thing
Brutus hated more than being
disturbed when he was napping:
the color red!

And that was precisely what
he saw when he stormed
out into the yard —

three fire-engine-red foxes!

Brutus galloped after them and made them howl and run for their lives.

Ralph knew that now the foxes were gone for good.
"Atta boy, Brutus!"
he called from the window.
"We did it!"

The danger was over. The rabbits climbed out of the cellar. When they found out what Ralph had done, they gave him a big cheer. Then the happy rabbits celebrated not only Liza's birthday, but also their good fortune.

Liza told everybody, "Ralph must be the greatest soccer player in the world. Nobody else could have made a kick like that."

After everyone had a piece of birthday cake,
they all played a great game of soccer.